W9-AZO-540

THE SEVEN DAYS OF KWANZAA

With love to Carol Crolle and all my friends
at Westfield Academy and Central School
—M.C.

To my Ruby and George
—J.T.

No part of this publication may be reproduced, stored in a retrieval system, or transmitted in
any form or by any means, electronic, mechanical, photocopying, recording, or otherwise, without
written permission of the publisher. For more information regarding permission, write to
Scholastic Inc., 557 Broadway, New York, NY 10012.

Text copyright © 2007 by Melrose Cooper.
Illustrations copyright © 2007 by Jeremy Tugeau.

All rights reserved. Published by Scholastic Inc. SCHOLASTIC, CARTWHEEL BOOKS,
and associated logos are trademarks and/or registered trademarks of Scholastic Inc.

ISBN-13: 978-0-439-56746-6
ISBN-10: 0-439-56746-7

Library of Congress Cataloging-in-Publication Data

Cooper, Melrose.
The seven days of Kwanzaa / by Melrose Cooper ; illustrated by Jeremy Tugeau.
p. cm.
"Cartwheel books."
Summary: This version of the popular holiday song celebrates the
culture, heritage, family, and tradition of Kwanzaa.
ISBN-13: 978-0-439-56746-6 (pbk.)
ISBN-10: 0-439-56746-7 (pbk.)
1. Children's songs, English--United States--Texts. [1. Kwanzaa--Songs
and music. 2. Songs.] I. Tugeau, Jeremy, ill. II. Title.
PZ8.3.C788Se 2007
782.42--dc22
[E]   2007001003

10 9 8 7 6 5 4 3 2 1   07 08 09 10 11

Printed in the U.S.A.
First printing October 2007

THE SEVEN DAYS OF KWANZAA

by Melrose Cooper

Illustrated by Jeremy Tugeau

Cartwheel
·B·O·O·K·S·®

SCHOLASTIC INC.

New York   Toronto   London   Auckland   Sydney
Mexico City   New Delhi   Hong Kong   Buenos Aires

On the first day of Kwanzaa,
my people gave to me . . .
A promise for unity.

Kujichagulia

On the second day of Kwanzaa, my people gave to me . . .

Two drums a-drumming
And a promise for unity.

Ujima

On the third day of Kwanzaa,
my people gave to me . . .

Red, green, and black,
Two drums a-drumming,
And a promise for unity.

Ujamaa

On the fourth day of Kwanzaa,
my people gave to me . . .
Four spending dollars,

Red, green, and black,
Two drums a-drumming,
And a promise for unity.

Nia

On the fifth day of Kwanzaa,
my people gave to me . . .
Five festive friends!

Four spending dollars,

Red, green,
and black,

Two drums a-drumming,

And a promise for unity.

On the sixth day of Kwanzaa,
my people gave to me . . .
Six handmade presents,

Five festive friends!

Four spending dollars,

Red, green,
and black,

Two drums a-drumming,

And a promise for unity.

Imani

On the seventh day of Kwanzaa,
my people gave to me . . .
Seven gleaming candles,

Six handmade presents,
Five festive friends!
Four spending dollars,

Red, green, and black,
Two drums a-drumming,

And a promise for unity.

Kwanzaa is an African-American holiday that celebrates history, culture, and customs, and has its roots in an African harvest festival. Music and drums are a part of the celebration, which includes dancing, feasting, and praying. Many folks dress in their fanciest, most colorful clothing, much of it African in design.

Three main colors are associated with Kwanzaa. Red represents the struggles the people have endured and the blood that has been shed. Green stands for fairness and justice and the lush African plant life. Black represents the people themselves. A *bendera*, or flag, that is used during Kwanzaa has three horizontal stripes of red, black, and green. A *kinara*, or candleholder, holds three red candles, three green candles, and one black.

For each of the seven days, one principle is celebrated—Unity, Control, Cooperation, Sharing of Profits, Purpose, Creativity, and Faith. Their names in the African language of Kiswahili are *Umoja, Kujichagulia, Ujima, Ujamaa, Nia, Kuumba,* and *Imani*.

Ears of corn are put out on a place mat to represent the children, and handmade gifts are often given, especially on the sixth day when creativity is highlighted.